Journey Inside the Computer

For Mom, obviously. And for Ville, who fell with me.

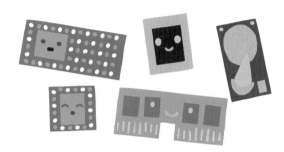

A FEIWEL AND FRIENDS BOOK
An Imprint of Macmillan Publishing Group, LLC

HELLO RUBY: JOURNEY INSIDE THE COMPUTER. Copyright © 2017 by Linda Liukas.
All rights reserved. Printed in China by RR Donnelley Asia Printing Solutions Ltd.,
Dongguan City, Guangdong Province.

For information, address Feiwel and Friends, 175 Fifth Avenue, New York, N.Y. 10010.
Our books may be purchased in bulk for promotional, educational, or business use. Please contact your local
bookseller or the Macmillan Corporate and Premium Sales Department at (800) 221-7945 ext. 5442 or by e-mail
at MacmillanSpecialMarkets@macmillan.com.

Library of Congress Cataloging-in-Publication Data is available.
ISBN 978-1-250-06532-2 (hardcover) / ISBN 978-1-250-13569-8 (ebook)

Book design by Eileen Savage
Feiwel and Friends logo designed by Filomena Tuosto
First Edition—2017
The artwork was created in Photoshop using brushes by Kyle T. Webster.
The Android robot is reproduced or modified from work created and shared by Google and
used according to terms described in the Creative Commons 3.0 Attribution License.

1 3 5 7 9 10 8 6 4 2

mackids.com

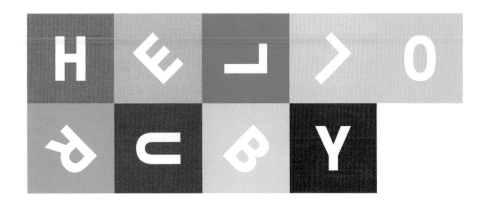

Journey Inside the Computer

Linda Liukas

Feiwel and Friends
New York

Introduction for the Parent

Our world is increasingly run by computers. But ask a person on the street how computers actually work, and you'll get no response.

The graphical interface, the sleek containers, and sealed boxes hide a lot of complexity from us. How do the bits and bytes come together inside the box? How does electricity turn into logic; how does logic create ones and zeroes? And how does all this link to the physical world of processors and memory chips?

As computers become more subtle, more complex, and ever so tiny, we've lost our understanding.

And it's not only the type of computers you and I recognize: the desktop, the tablet, the mobile phone. This generation of kids will be the last to remember the computer as the glowing box. They will grow up in a world where computers are everywhere, from their teddy bears to their toothbrushes.

So how do we talk to kids about computers? What are the mental models and metaphors we use?

This story is an attempt to familiarize kids with the computer. It's not a textbook or reference on how to build a computer. Thorough understanding of how computers work is a rabbit hole of learning. This is a story about one imaginative way of seeing computers, of breaking that glossy, mysterious container and showing what's hidden underneath.

A few practical tips: The toolboxes are intended for parents and give additional information on the topic. Throughout the activity book the reader will be building a paper computer. There are always activities that relate to building a computer, but also discussions, games, and printable exercises. You can find suggested answers at helloruby .com/answers. Don't rush through the activities; stop and wonder together. Some kids will be interested in learning more about logic gates. For others, it's enough to hear the terms.

A century and a half ago, Lewis Carroll plunged his Alice into a fantastical world through the rabbit hole. I'm sending Ruby on a similar mission from the operating systems to the tiniest bits—and everything in between.

Ruby and Her Friends

Ruby

About me: I like learning new things and I hate giving up. I love to share my opinions. Want to hear a few? My dad is the best. I tell great jokes. And I have five special gemstones.

Secret Superpower: I can imagine impossible things.

Favorite Expression: Why?

Pet Peeves: I hate confusion.

Bits

About us: We are the tiniest members of the family and always answer yes or no. Our interests include punch cards, magnets, electricity, and coins.

Secret Superpower: We calculate in a very special way: 8, 16, 32, 64, 128, 256. Isn't it funny?

Favorite Expression: Kibibit! Mebibit! Pebibit!

Pet Peeves: Things that are stuck or in between

Logic Gates

About us: We are holders of the truth. We are always exact, but sometimes a little repetitious. We work together with others but get into arguments easily.

Secret Superpower: We can tell what is true and what is false.

Favorite Expression: Truth!

Pet Peeves: Quantum logic

THE SOFTWARE DEPARTMENT

Cursor

About me: I'm quick and a bit of a jester. Sometimes I bounce around uncontrollably.

Secret Superpower: I like to change my outfit depending on the occasion. Sometimes I'm a pointing arrow, sometimes a dragging hand, sometimes a skinny pointer.

Favorite Expression: Always look at the world a bit tilted!

Pet Peeves: Too-small boxes, beach balls, hourglasses

Snow Leopard

About me: I'm the most beautiful, polite, and well-mannered Snow Leopard I know. I often have fights with the Robots. (Which is kind of pointless, since we are similar in the end.)

Secret Superpower: Boundless beauty

Favorite Expression: Think different.

Pet Peeves: People think I'm tough, but I'm really cuddly.

Mouse

About me: I'm an eager beaver and like to help. I'm an efficient friend of the computer. Sometimes I have a tail or even blue teeth!

Secret Superpower:	The right button
Favorite Expression:	Does it click?
Pet Peeves:	I don't like touchscreens.

RAM

About me: I work together with the CPU, GPU, and Mass Storage, but I forget everything once you close the computer.

Secret Superpower:	I'm fast and flexible.
Favorite Expression:	Swap, your turn!
Pet Peeves:	Memory errors and leaks

ROM

About me: I keep hold of everything you don't want to accidentally remove. Otherwise I sleep. You might also know my cousin Flash.

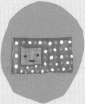

Secret Superpower:	I forget nothing.
Favorite Expression:	Wake up!
Pet Peeves:	I'm very small, old, and quite slow. But still important.

GPU

About me: I handle everything related to forming a picture on the screen.

Secret Superpower:	I can do many things simultaneously. I'm often faster than the processor.
Favorite Expression:	Faster!
Pet Peeves:	Pixels

CPU

About me: It's up to me how fast and effectively the computer works. You can find me in many places—everywhere from mobile phones to space rockets!

Secret Superpower:	Number crunching
Favorite Expression:	Fetch! Decode! Execute!
Pet Peeves:	I heat up easily; luckily there's the fan.

Mass Storage

About me: I hold everything in order.

Secret Superpower:	I'm the biggest of them all.
Favorite Expression:	Oh, memories!
Pet Peeves:	Clouds

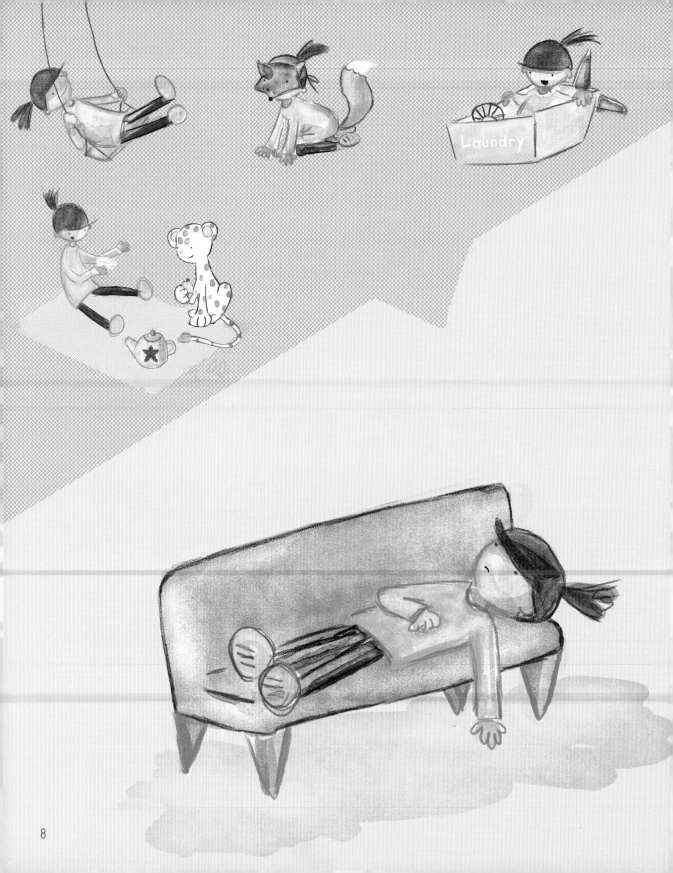

Chapter 1: Boring

Ruby is a small girl with a huge imagination. Anything is possible if Ruby puts her mind to it. But today Ruby is bored.

There is nothing to do and nobody to play with.
No fun tea parties to go to, no rafts to build.
Even the toys are just sitting and staring.
"Doesn't seem like an adventure," Ruby sighs.

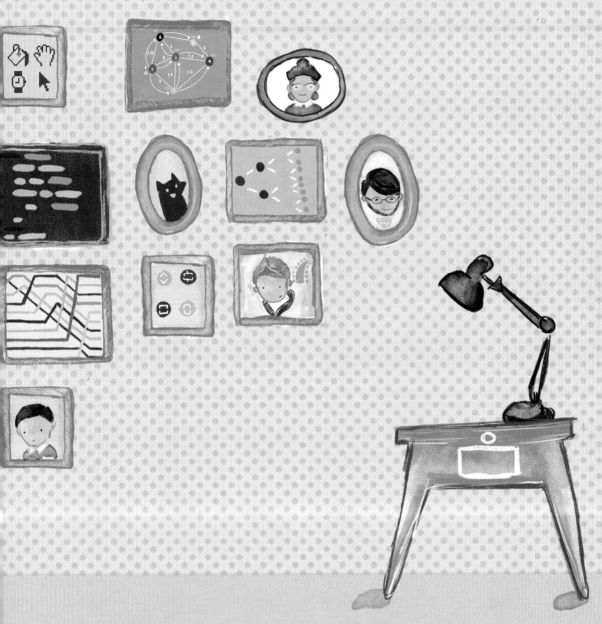

Dad had promised Ruby they would play together with the computer, but now he isn't home.

"Dad made a promise. I'll just go and play with the computer all by myself," Ruby says as she marches to his office.

Chapter 2: Dad's Computer

Ruby turns on the computer and the screen lights up. She carefully types the password, "littlemissruby1010," and clicks. Nothing happens. Ruby clicks the mouse again and wiggles it a bit.

"Silly computer," Ruby mutters.

All of a sudden the little white Mouse sniffs and says, "The computer isn't working today."

"What's wrong?"

"Cursor isn't answering my messages," Mouse says. "Cursor and I always work as a team. But now he's gone missing."

Ruby thinks this is starting to sound like an adventure.

"Well, I just happen to be the best computer troubleshooter I know. I can help you find your friend."

MOUSE HOLE

"Thank you. I've already
tried everything I can
think of! Follow me; I know how we can get into the
computer," says Mouse. "This is how I send messages
into the computer."

A mouse hole! Ruby has never noticed the holes on
the side of the computer.

All excited, she makes herself very small and crawls
after Mouse.

And then she falls.

Chapter 3: Electricity and Bits

Downward and inward Ruby falls until she finally lands in a big hall with billions of glittering little bits.

"It's dazzling." Ruby exhales. "What's happening here?"

"Oh, they are bits. They go on and off, on and off, all the time. Everything in a computer is built on bits."

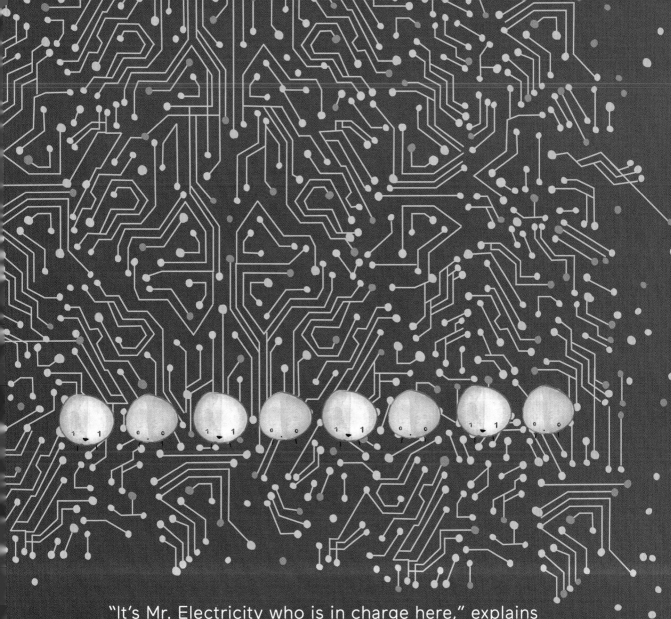

"It's Mr. Electricity who is in charge here," explains Mouse.

"Should we start looking for Cursor?" Ruby suggests.

"Bits won't be any help. Trying to talk directly with bits is too tiresome. They only talk in ones and zeroes and it takes at least eight of them working together to say anything more than yes or no. We need to get to the next level," Mouse answers impatiently.

Chapter 4: Logic Gates

Ruby and Mouse climb up the ladder and peek over the top.

Mouse points out a door in the far wall. "Through there we should be able to get some help."

But there is a series of strange formations and gates in the way.

Ruby and Mouse try to sneak quietly past them, but they are spotted!

"Hi there! If you want to go through the gates, you have to solve our riddles first. Answer either TRUE or FALSE. We practice logic and reason all the time!"

Ruby is prepared to take up the challenge.
She marches up to the first gate.

I have eyes
AND a mouth.

True!

I am NOT
green.

True!

I have legs
OR a tail.

False!

"Very good, Ruby! Now we can play another game. It's called EXCLUSIVE OR."
"No, Ruby, let's run. We'll take the shortcut," Mouse whispers.

Chapter 5: Computer Architecture

"I know who we can ask for help," says Mouse. "The CPU. But he's very bossy and I'm afraid to interrupt him."

Even from afar, they can hear someone shouting commands.

"FETCH, DECODE, STORE, NEXT!"

Ruby walks straight up to the CPU and tries to act very professional.

"Are you the boss here?"

"Yes. I am the CPU of the computer. I tell others what to do. I'm very fast and right now I'm extremely busy."

"Mr. CPU, Cursor isn't working today. Have you seen him around?"

The CPU looks confused.

"I don't know. It's not my job to remember everything! I'm very busy making decisions. You'd better talk to GPU. Cursor is her assistant."

"Welcome. Come look at my beautiful creations. My secret is mathematical precision." GPU exhales.

"No sign of Cursor here," says Mouse.

"Here comes RAM; let's ask her," says Mouse.
RAM is panting. "I'm so hot."
"So why are you running all the time?" asks Ruby.
"CPU and GPU keep bossing me. It's always me who needs to fetch every little detail from Mass Storage," says RAM, and continues running.

"We have a problem. Cursor has been missing all day," explains Ruby. "Do you remember what happened?"

"Check Mass Storage. He remembers everything. At the end of the day I'm exhausted and my head is all empty."

Ruby walks up to Mass Storage.

"Ruby, you won't find Cursor here in the hardware department. You'll need to go to the software department," he explains, sounding very friendly and wise.

File Edit View

RUBY

```
1   {$S        }
2   ...CursorNormal;
3   BEGIN
4     InitC...          not hidden }
5     GridMou...              }
6   END;
7
8   {$S
9   ...
10  TYPE crsrPtr...
11       crsrHnd...
12  VAR  hou...         ;
13  BEGIN
14    ...ouse(...    { no grid  }
15    ...orFlag...
    ...ourGlass...     ...RD(GetCursor(4)));
```

●● ▶
SOFTWARE

Chapter 6: Software

Onward and upward they go.

"This looks familiar," says Ruby. "Look, that's my favorite game!"

"This is where Cursor should be," Mouse worries.

"Hello, Ruby! Oh, and great that you came, Mouse,"
says Snow Leopard. "I'm having a little tea party
here. It's been such a quiet day today. Have you seen
Cursor, by any chance? It's very difficult to use my
operating system without Cursor."

"We are here to find Cursor. But asking around
hasn't helped us. We must now do troubleshooting
to solve this problem," says Ruby with a determined
look on her face.

HARDWARE

SUDO

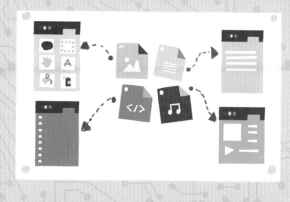

PROCESSOR

DEVICES

SECURITY

MEMORY

FILES

UTILITIES

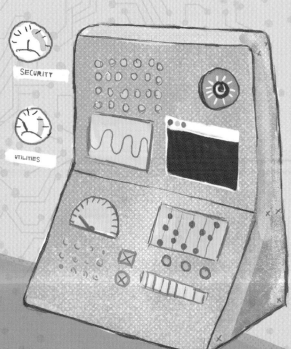

SOFTWARE

```
{$S         }
PROCEDURE CursorNormal;
BEGIN
   InitCursor;                  arrow, not hidden }
   GridMouse(-1,-1,0,0);        no grid  }
END;


{$S         }
PROCEDURE BusyCursor;
TYPE crsrPtr  = ^Cursor;
     crsrHndl = ^CrsrPtr;
VAR  hourGlass: crsrHndl;
BEGIN
   GridMouse(-1,-1,0,0);      { no grid }
   cursorFlag := TRUE;
   hourGlass := Pointer(ORD(GetCursor(4)));
   SetCursor(hourGlass^^);
END;
```

Chapter 7: Troubleshoot

"First, we'll think of all the places where Cursor might be.

   "Next, we'll rule out the places where we've already
visited and didn't find Cursor.

"And if that doesn't work, we'll have to think why Cursor is missing. The best troubleshooters always ask why," Ruby says knowingly.

"Aha! I think I know what happened," Ruby says after a moment, while plugging Mouse into the computer.

And finally Ruby finds Cursor fast asleep.

"Mouse! What a long nap. I must have fallen
asleep while waiting for something to happen."
Cursor yawns and stands up. "We better start
clicking, spinning, pushing, dragging, dropping,
and pointing."

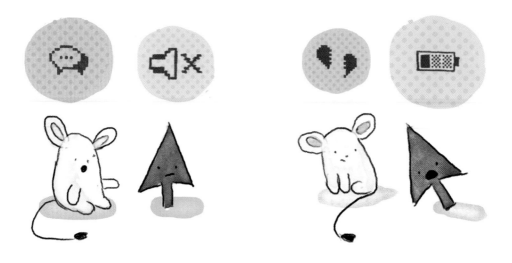

Mouse smiles and
wiggles its tail.

"Mouse and Cursor, you make such a great team, and now you can continue working together," says Ruby. "I'm such a good troubleshooter. Dad will be so proud to see how well the computer now works."

Activity Book

Hi.

My name is Ruby, and computers are the most exciting thing I know. And now you'll get to design your very own computer. You'll also learn many wonderful things about your new computer.

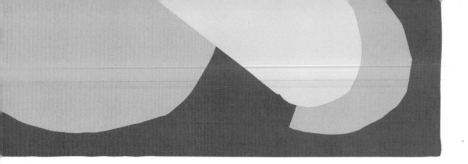

What you'll need:

- 2 pieces of paper

- Scissors

- Tape and glue

- Brightly colored pens or pencils

- Scrap paper for decoration

FOLLOW THIS ICON TO BUILD YOUR OWN COMPUTER.

Instructions

1. Start by taking out a piece of paper and folding it in half. Be careful and precise. Turn the page and study the computer parts shown.
2. Draw the motherboard and the spaces for the components according to the instructions.
3. Next, take the other piece of paper and draw the components on the next page. Cut out the components. Put them aside in a neat pile to wait for exercise 12.
4. Use what's left of the other piece of paper to design the keyboard. Measure your computer to make sure it fits. Cut it out.
5. Copy and cut out the operating systems, files, stickers, and the website.
6. Ta-da! You're ready to go.

Build Your Computer

These are the parts of the computer you should draw on your paper.

Computer case and Motherboard

Start by copying the casing of the computer on the first paper. Notice the yellow boxes. This is where code in exercise 20 goes.

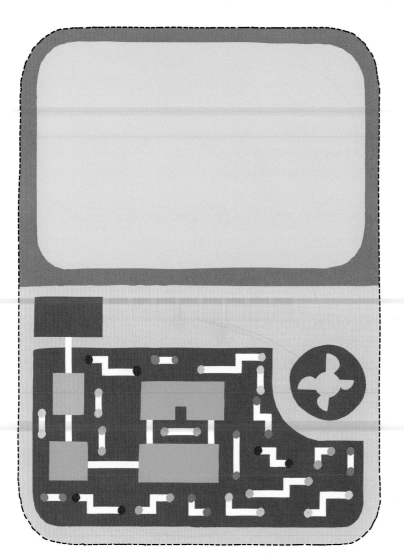

Components

Copy the components onto another piece of paper. Write down the names.

RAM

HARD DRIVE

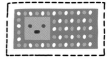

ROM

CPU

GPU

Operating system

These are the operating system logos.
Draw them, too!

Website

Make an extra website.

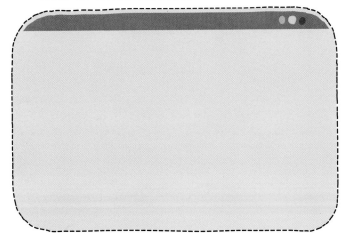

Keyboard

Copy the keyboard carefully. Remember the on/off button!

Stickers

These are ideas for stickers you can use to decorate your computer. But you can make your own!

Files

Copy files for your desktop.

 You can also print and cut out this computer at **helloruby.com/computer**

1

WHAT IS A COMPUTER?

Computers make great friends. A computer lets you draw images, listen to songs, create games, and calculate impossibly big numbers. Ruby met both the hardware and software families. Now it's your turn.

Toolbox:

Computers are built with hardware and software. The electrical or mechanical parts of a computer are called hardware. The instructions and the programs inside the computer are the software. Hardware and software work together to run a computer.

You'll see the hardware when you open the computer.

Name Your Computer

Turn your computer around. Give it a name and a serial number. You can name your computer anything. The serial number is what makes the computer unique. And who built the computer? Sign your work!

Have you met my famous computer friends ENIAC, Lisa, Watson, and HAL?

Name

Serial number

Engineer

Hardware or Software?

Ruby's new friends have different families. Mouse belongs to hardware, whereas Cursor is software. They work great together. Look at the pictures. Which ones are hardware? Which ones are software? And which ones belong together?

Phone

Pointer

Game console

Chat application

Word processing application

Game

Printer

Hello world!

Mouse

Is This a Computer?

Computers are everywhere. You probably have more than a hundred computers at home.

Which of these objects are computers? Which ones are not?

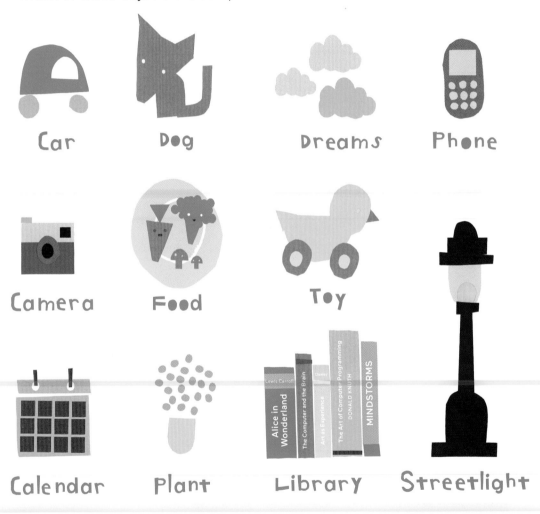

Car   Dog   Dreams   Phone

Camera   Food   Toy

Calendar   Plant   Library   Streetlight

 Discuss

Ask an adult which of these objects was a computer ten years ago. Imagine together which ones of these might turn into computers in ten years.

2

WHAT ARE COMPUTERS USED FOR?

Computers are helpful in many ways. They are fast, accurate, and good at repeating things. You can find computers in many places. Ruby used Dad's desktop computer. But computers can also look very different.

Toolbox:

Computers might look like they are doing complicated things, but all they do is a huge number of simple calculations one after another very fast.

Computers don't come up with solutions on their own: They need instructions to follow. People, on the other hand, can think creatively and independently. That's why the two make such a great team.

Do you remember me?

Assemble Your Computer

Take out your computer and add the keyboard under the screen. Use tape to fasten it on one side. This way you can always peek inside. You just made a laptop! Booyah!

Computers cannot think. Computers only do what they are told to do.

 Discuss

Better together! Draw a situation where you did something together with someone else! How could a computer help you?

How Do You Recognize a Computer?

Computers and humans are good at different things. Make a cheat sheet.

I'm good at:

My computer is good at:

I'm not so good at:

My computer is
not so good at:

After doing this
exercise, I feel:

After doing this exercise,
my computer feels:

My Computer Safari

Spot a computer! List all the computers you see during the week.

How to spot a computer? Look for clues like an on/off button, a cord, batteries, or a blinking light.

DAY	TIME	PLACE SPOTTED	WHAT DID THE COMPUTER DO?

THIS IS HOW MANY COMPUTERS I SPOTTED

 Print the Computer Safari form at **helloruby.com/play**

3

INPUT/OUTPUT MACHINE

Ruby falls inside the computer, but usually the only thing computers take in is data. When you type on a computer, the computer gets an input. Then the data is processed and the output shows the result on the screen.

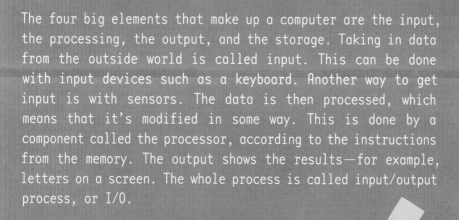

Toolbox:

The four big elements that make up a computer are the input, the processing, the output, and the storage. Taking in data from the outside world is called input. This can be done with input devices such as a keyboard. Another way to get input is with sensors. The data is then processed, which means that it's modified in some way. This is done by a component called the processor, according to the instructions from the memory. The output shows the results—for example, letters on a screen. The whole process is called input/output process, or I/O.

Memory

Take cupcakes out of the oven.

Frost each cupcake with your favorite flavor.

Gather your decorations.

Sprinkle decorations.

Input

▼

Process

▼

Output

Input or Output?

Which of these devices are for input? Which ones are for output? At least one device can be both.

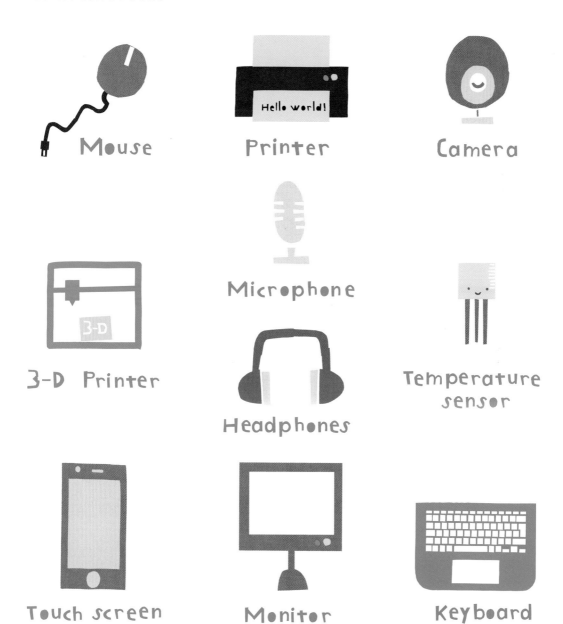

Mouse

Printer

Camera

Microphone

3-D Printer

Headphones

Temperature sensor

Touch screen

Monitor

Keyboard

Exercise 8

Make a Keyboard

A keyboard is an input device that is used to type text, numbers, and instructions for the computer.

First copy the letters onto your keyboard. You can model it after the keyboard on the next page. A keyboard is used with two hands. This is called typing. Can you write your own name with the keyboard? Practice typing with your index fingers.

Some keys have special skills.

Enter Key. Enter key can do many things! It can, for example, be pressed any time a button or choice is highlighted to tell the computer you select that particular item.

Backspace Key. Pressing this key will remove the character to the left of the cursor when pressed.

Space Bar. This key is used to enter a blank space between words.

Add numbers to your keyboard. How would you type 21 with the computer?

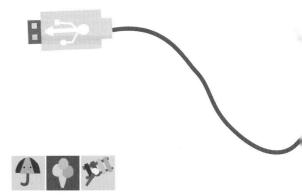

Design a new key! There are a few empty keys on the keyboard. Can you design your own key? What does your button do?

Finish by typing END.

Exercise 9

Design Your Input/Output Device

What if you could design a new type of input device, like a helmet or a pair of glasses? Or an output device, like a tiny projector? How would it look? Make it out of paper.

Let's make input and output devices for our computer. Draw or make out of paper extra items for your computer, like a mouse, a speaker, or a video camera.

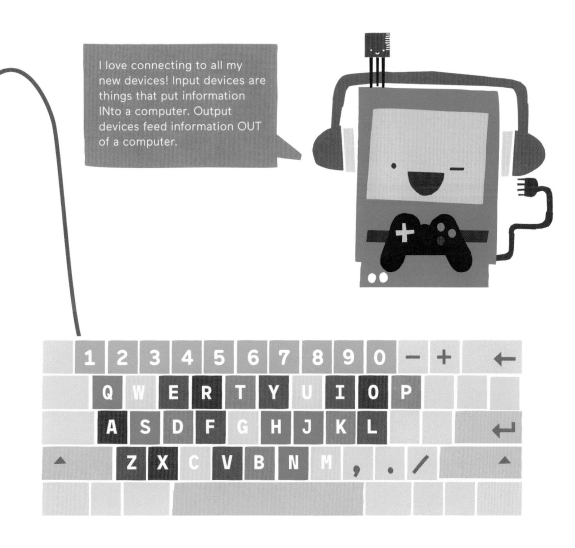

I love connecting to all my new devices! Input devices are things that put information INto a computer. Output devices feed information OUT of a computer.

How to Make Sense?

People can touch, hear, see, taste, and smell. Computers don't have hands, eyes, or a nose, but instead they have sensors that help them to collect input data from the world. Many phones have sensors.

1. Start by connecting each human body part to the right sense.

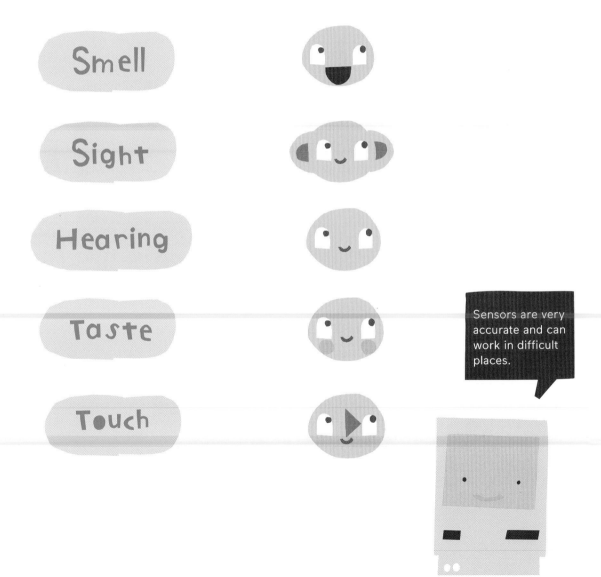

Smell

Sight

Hearing

Taste

Touch

Sensors are very accurate and can work in difficult places.

2. What are the ways a computer can sense the world around it? Can you think of a new sensor for your computer? What would it do? Fill your ideas in on the chart below.

Sensor	what it detects	How a sensor can affect your computer
Temperature	Measures how hot or cool something is and the changes in temperature.	Your computer can recognize when it's cold outside and remind you to put on more clothes.
Light	Recognizes changes in the amount of light, like morning or evening.	
Pressure	Recognizes changes in pressure, like if you're sitting on a chair or pushing a button.	
Moisture	Recognizes changes in the moisture, like if it's raining outside.	
Movement	Recognizes changes in movement, for instance if someone walks in the door.	

The Incredible I/O Machine

Let's practice input-process-output together. Fill in the missing actions from the process.

1. Example: Practice calculating with the computer. Follow the computer's actions with your finger.

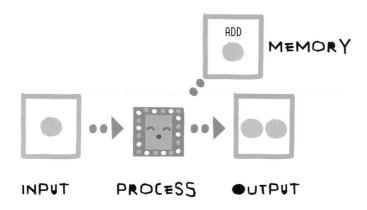

2. Can you help the processor? How many pink circles did the processing add?

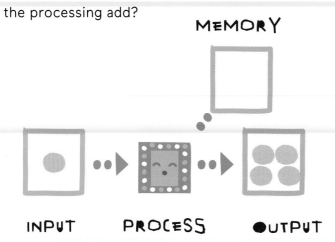

3. What about here—how many pink circles were input originally?

MEMORY

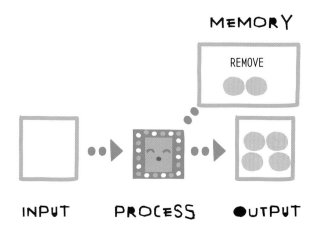

REMOVE

INPUT   PROCESS   ●OUTPUT

4. What happens when you send a story to a printer?
Describe the output.

MEMORY

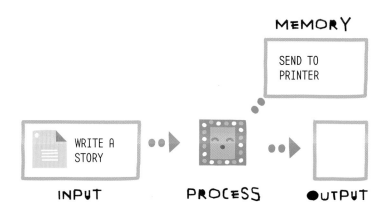

SEND TO
PRINTER

WRITE A
STORY

INPUT   PROCESS   ●OUTPUT

Computers can only process data
when it's turned into bits. That's
why each click or tap is turned into
ones and zeroes.

5. Car. Even new cars have computers inside them! What kind of sensor helps notice if someone is sitting in the seat? What happens if the seat belt is unfastened? Describe the output.

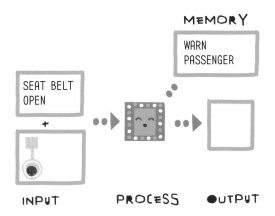

MEMORY

WARN PASSENGER

SEAT BELT OPEN

+

INPUT   PROCESS   ●OUTPUT

6. Garden. How can a light sensor and a moisture sensor help you in a garden? Describe the process.

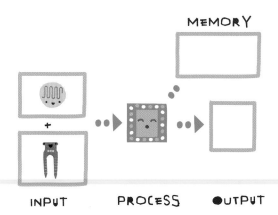

MEMORY

+

INPUT   PROCESS   ●OUTPUT

💬 Discuss

Together with an adult, use the input-process-output model to describe the following things. Describe what happens:
- Paying in a store with a credit card
- Setting off a smoke alarm
- Sending an e-mail
- Using a microwave
- Can you come up with your own example?

4

WHAT ARE THE MAIN PARTS INSIDE A COMPUTER?

Remember the busy components Ruby met? Inside the computer there are lots of small electronic components. Each one of the components has a special role.

Toolbox:

The computer Ruby explores is a desktop. But if you look inside your mobile phone, many of the components work the same. They might look a little different or lack certain parts, but most of them are designed with the same principle, which is known as the Von Neumann architecture.

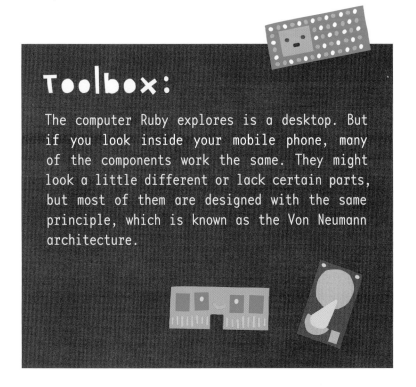

The more the merrier! Computers are made of many, many small components!

Exercise 12

Add the Components

Make sure to place all your components in the right place on the mother-board! The motherboard is the heart of the computer. Every important component either sits here or connects to it.

The buses connect the components inside the motherboard and help the data move inside. Find an open bus to the fan inside the motherboard.

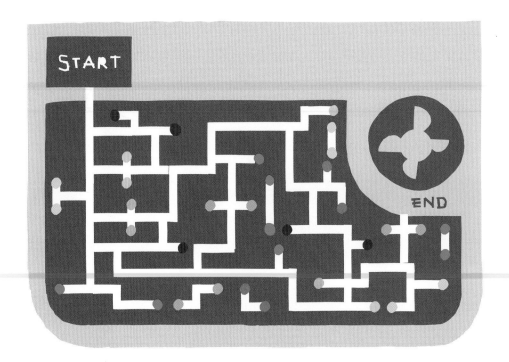

Computer Memory Game. At **helloruby.com/play** you can print pictures of the different parts of the computer and make your own memory game cards.

Connect the Components

Can you guess who is who? Follow the same color to connect the different components with the right name.

GPU
(Graphics Processing Unit)

I focus on showing things on the computer screen. I'm good at calculating.

CPU
(Central Processing Unit)

I am very smart and fast at calculating things. I am super busy bossing around and telling other components what to do, but I have a bad memory.

Mass Storage

I'm like a drawer where you can put things in and they stay here. I usually have lots of space, but I'm very slow.

RAM
(Random Access Memory)

I remember all immediate things and run between the CPU and Mass Storage. I'm very fast. But everything that is stored in RAM disappears when you close your computer.

ROM
(Read Only Memory)

When the computer is switched on, it is my job to figure out who should do what and get them up and running. After that I rest.

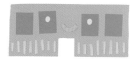

Challenge the GPU

The GPU is in charge of calculating what your computer screen shows. Can you challenge the GPU?

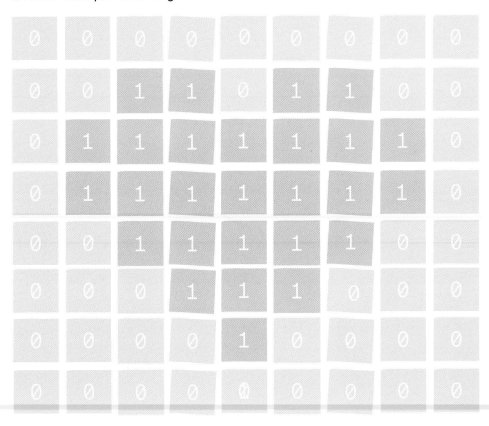

- Count how many ones there are in the picture. And what about zeroes?
- Is the fourth symbol on the second row counting from left a one or a zero?
- What is the shape that is formed in the picture?
- What does the shape usually mean? What kind of feelings do you have?

My GPU can count this in a nanosecond!

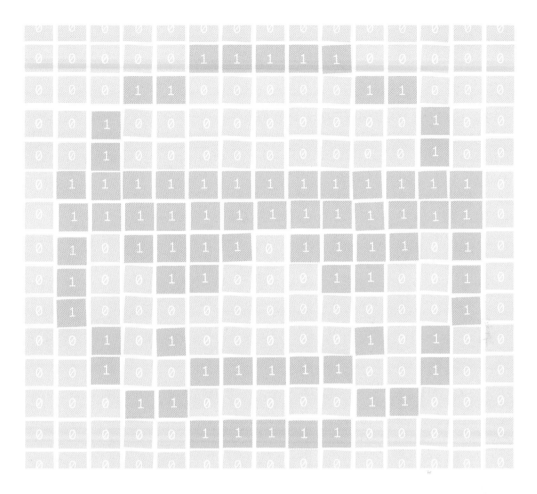

- Count how many ones there are in the picture. And what about zeroes?
- Is the fourth symbol on the second row counting from left a one or a zero?
- What is the shape that is formed in the picture?
- What does the shape usually mean? What kind of feelings do you have?

 # Discuss

Who wins the competition? Which one of these exercises is easy for people? What about for computers? Go back to exercise 5 for hints.

Chip Sudoku

The chips inside a computer are made of small electronic components like amplifiers, resistors, and transistors. Help Ruby design four chips. Fill each chip so that each row and each column have only one of the same component. Use all the components.

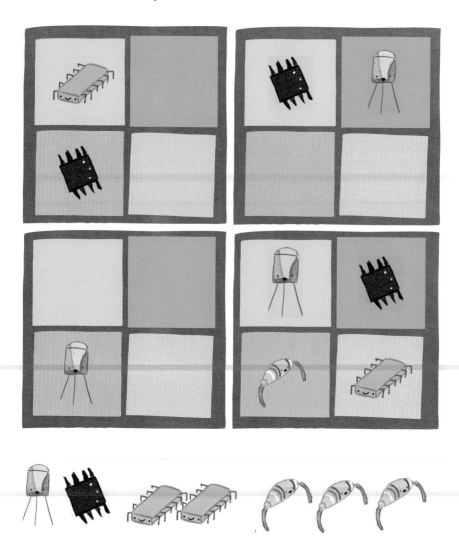

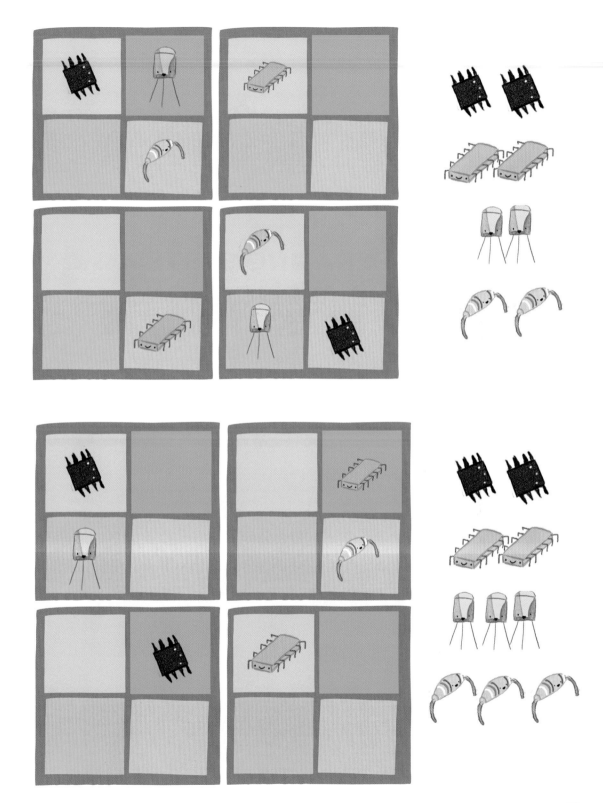

5

OPERATING SYSTEM AND APPLICATIONS

When Ruby moves to the operating system, things start to look familiar. All computers have an operating system that makes it easy to use a computer. Applications are used to do specific tasks on a computer, such as writing an e-mail, making a poster, or messaging friends.

Toolbox:

The operating system (OS) is like a traffic cop. It passes instructions between the software and the hardware, handles memory, and makes sure things happen seamlessly. The operating system also manages all the applications. Applications are usually designed specifically for each operating system. Operating systems often use symbols like files and folders to help you use your computer, but some operating systems are text based.

Operating systems make using a computer simple. Without an operating system we would need to talk in the computer's own language of ones and zeroes.

Common Operating Systems

Pick your operating system and add the logo to the back of the computer.
On some computers it's possible to run more than one operating system.

Linux
Linux is built by people all around the world.

macOS
macOS is used in Mac computers.

Windows
Windows is the very popular operating
system created by Microsoft.

Other popular operating systems include **Android** and **iOS** (for smartphones).
They are designed for touchscreen devices.

> Operating systems are huge programs: Windows
> Vista is rumored to have around 50 million lines
> of code; MacOSX 86 million. Can you imagine
> how many books that would fill?

 ## Discuss

Why did you choose this operating system
for your computer?

Exercise 16

Design Your Own OS

Different operating systems share a lot of things. Now it's your turn to build an operating system for a phone. Copy the phone template from the picture on the right. You can draw inspiration from an existing operating system or come up with something of your own.

Applications

- What kind of apps does your phone have? Design the icons on the home screen.
- Draw your own background image.
- Design an application on the application screen. You can use the elements below.

Functionalities

- What happens when someone calls your phone? Design the view.
- How does your phone take pictures? How do you view the pictures?
- What kind of keyboard does your phone have? Does it have emoji?

Home View:

App View:

 You can print out more phone templates
at **helloruby.com/play**

 # Discuss

Can you make an operating system with only text?
What would an operating system for a watch look
like? What about a fridge? A spacecraft?

6
BITS, LOGIC GATES, AND ELECTRICITY

The first things Ruby ran into inside the computer were bits. Inside a computer, at a very low level, everything is simply a bunch of switches that are ON or OFF. These are called bits. Your computer is really good at pretending there are photographs, stories, and songs inside it. But it's all just electricity!

Toolbox:

Electricity is the flow of electrons around a circuit. When you turn on the computer, electricity flows into the chips. If there is no electricity in the bit, the bit is OFF. When electricity is present, then the bit is ON. Binary is a word we use to describe being in a state of one of two conditions. Computer scientists use the numbers one and zero. In logic it's called true or false.

ELECTRICITY	BINARY	BOOLEAN
ON	1	TRUE
OFF	0	FALSE

Design Your Own Power Plug

The power supply unit takes the electricity from the wall and divides it among the different components. In a laptop, it's situated outside of the computer.

Design a power plug with paper and string for your computer to connect it!

Computer devices are often connected with cords. In addition to electricity, the cords transfer data. Can you connect the right cord to the right device? Explain what happens when the cord is connected.

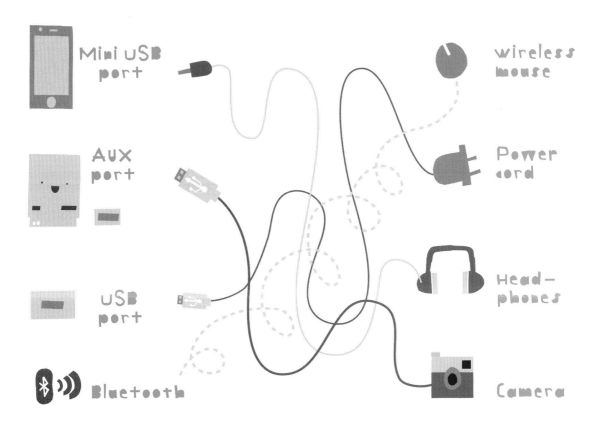

Mini USB port

Aux port

USB port

Bluetooth

wireless mouse

Power cord

Head-phones

Camera

 **Discuss**

Can you see electricity?

Think Like a Computer

Having only two options might not seem like a lot. But you can communicate quite a bit with only two digits.

0 = NO	1 = YES

Together with a friend, think of one of the following friends: CPU, GPU, RAM, ROM, Mass Storage, and Mouse. Try to figure out who's who by asking only questions you can answer yes or no to! Take turns.

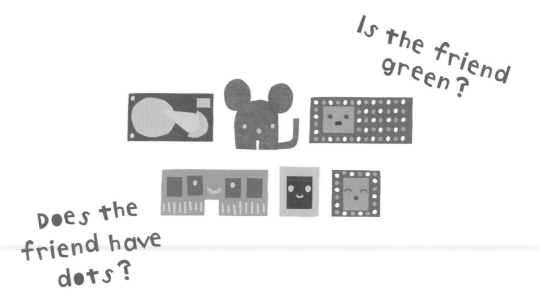

Is the friend green?

Does the friend have dots?

Discuss

Can you have a real discussion with only yes and no? Try it out!
- What was your friend's favorite birthday present last year?
- What did they have for breakfast in the morning?
- What's their favorite color?

How Much Is One Bit?

A bit is a unit of measure, just like an inch, a minute, a kilogram, or a meter. The different ways in which the bits are put together have special names. Eight bits is one byte.

Which of these files do you think will take up the most space? Connect the right item with the right size. You can investigate together with an adult using real files.

One byte

A holiday picture

One gigabyte

The letter A

A group of 8 bits is a byte. A thousand bites makes a kilobyte. A thousand kilobytes make a megabyte. A thousand megabytes make a gigabyte.

One kilobyte

One paragraph of text

One megabyte

A short video

Write Like a Computer

Yes (1) and no (0) will get you only so far. Another way to use binary is to come up with a special code for each letter of the alphabet. With only eight digits, a computer can have the entire alphabet with lower and uppercase as well as numbers and punctuation symbols. Pretty good for only two digits!

Find the first letter of the name you gave to your computer and write it in binary in the space above the motherboard.

Can you write your name in binary?

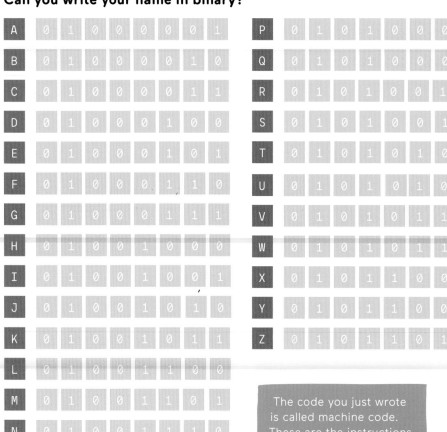

A	0	1	0	0	0	0	0	1
B	0	1	0	0	0	0	1	0
C	0	1	0	0	0	0	1	1
D	0	1	0	0	0	1	0	0
E	0	1	0	0	0	1	0	1
F	0	1	0	0	0	1	1	0
G	0	1	0	0	0	1	1	1
H	0	1	0	0	1	0	0	0
I	0	1	0	0	1	0	0	1
J	0	1	0	0	1	0	1	0
K	0	1	0	0	1	0	1	1
L	0	1	0	0	1	1	0	0
M	0	1	0	0	1	1	0	1
N	0	1	0	0	1	1	1	0
O	0	1	0	0	1	1	1	1
P	0	1	0	1	0	0	0	0
Q	0	1	0	1	0	0	0	1
R	0	1	0	1	0	0	1	0
S	0	1	0	1	0	0	1	1
T	0	1	0	1	0	1	0	0
U	0	1	0	1	0	1	0	1
V	0	1	0	1	0	1	1	0
W	0	1	0	1	0	1	1	1
X	0	1	0	1	1	0	0	0
Y	0	1	0	1	1	0	0	1
Z	0	1	0	1	1	0	1	0

The code you just wrote is called machine code. These are the instructions a CPU follows.

Who's Tricking You?

The logic gates are quite the puzzlers. Help Ruby solve which ones are lying.

AND gate

True 1	False 0

I am
Pink **AND** Green.

True 1	False 0

I am
Yellow **AND** Green.

True 1	False 0

I am.
Yellow **AND** Red.

True 1	False 0

I am.
Pink **AND** Yellow.

Computers make decisions using billions of tiny devices called logic gates. Logic gates have two kinds of output: ones that are TRUE and ones that are FALSE. There are three types of logic gates: AND, OR, and NOT. Now, when you combine these different kinds of logic gates, you can create super-complicated things like structures that run a streaming video or a drive a car.

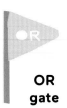

OR
gate

True 1	False 0

I am
Violet **OR** Pink.

True 1	False 0

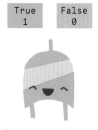

I am
Red **OR** Yellow.

True 1	False 0

I am
Red **OR** Pink.

True 1	False 0

I am
Violet **OR** Yellow.

NOT
gate

True 1	False 0

I am
NOT Yellow.

True 1	False 0

I am
NOT Blue.

True 1	False 0

I am
NOT Pink.

True 1	False 0

I am
NOT Violet.

Discuss

Look at the colors of each logic gate and see if they match the word underneath. Then write down whether the little logic gate was lying or not. Finally, fill in "true" or "false" into the table. The first one is filled in as an example. You just made a truth table!

Inputs		Output
True	True	True

Inputs		Output
False	False	False

Input	Output
False	True

For me, TRUE = 1 and FALSE = 0.

87

7

GOING THROUGH YOUR COMPUTER

Yay! You did it. You built your own computer. You added input/output devices, put the components in place, chose an operating system, gave your computer a name, wrote machine code, and designed a power plug. Now it's time to put it in use!

Awesome work!

Toolbox:

Modern computers are examples of collaborative creativity: Engineers, electronics experts, psychologists, physicists, material scientists, and many other professions needed to come together to create the computer—there is no one father or mother. Computers are still in their infancy and it's up to all of us to help them grow by using them as enablers of creativity. Every profession will benefit from being familiar with and unafraid of computers.

Electricity and logic make a magical pair!

Applications

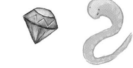

Operating system

Programming languages

Chips

Components

Logic gates

Bits and
electricity

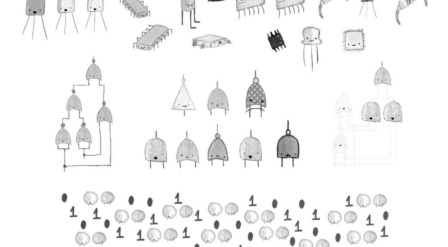

What Can You Do with a Computer?

Design an application for your computer or for a mobile phone.

1. BRAINSTORM

First, start by thinking about what kind of problems an app can help solve.
How could a computer help the following people?

Chef   Game designer

Detective   You   Veterinarian

Mom   Grandfather   Journalist

Astronaut

2. MAKE A PROTOTYPE

Now, let's focus on one of your app ideas. In a sentence or
two, describe the app.

A prototype is just a test to help
you learn more about your idea.

3. DESIGN YOUR APP

You can use exercise 16 for help. Use your imagination
and all the skills you've learned.

Future Computer

You have just designed a laptop computer, but in the future computers will look very different.

From the following lists, choose one item from the yellow boxes and one sensor from the blue boxes. Imagine what the combination could do as a computer.

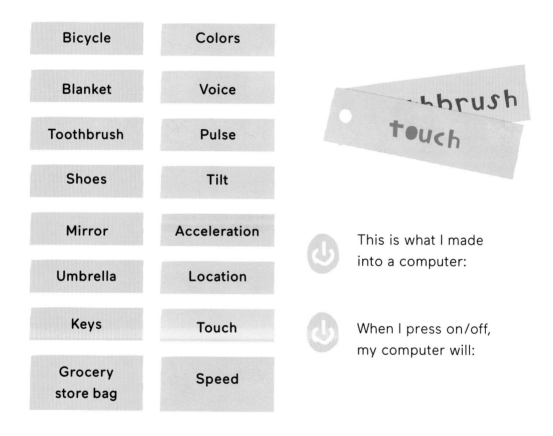

Bicycle	Colors
Blanket	Voice
Toothbrush	Pulse
Shoes	Tilt
Mirror	Acceleration
Umbrella	Location
Keys	Touch
Grocery store bag	Speed

This is what I made into a computer:

When I press on/off, my computer will:

Discuss

Ask an adult about their first computer. Compare it to your first experience of computers.

Follow the Computer Click

When you are using a computer to open a photo, there are thousands of tiny requests happening inside your computer. Follow the path with your finger and discover all the things that happen before the computer can show the photo onscreen.

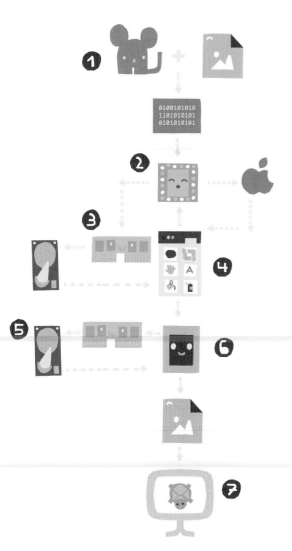

1. The mouse click generates code that tells the image it should be opened. The code generates an interruption in the CPU.

2. INTERRUPTION! Everyone stop what you're doing! The CPU passes the code on to the Operating System. The Operating System decides which application should open the file, but it needs the help of the Processor.

3. Processor instructs RAM to fetch the right application from the Mass Storage.

4. The photo application knows how to handle code like this. It needs the help of the GPU.

5. The GPU asks RAM to fetch the image from Mass Storage.

6. The GPU calculates which pixels on the monitor should be shaded in which way to create the picture.

7. Finally the picture is shown onscreen.

Guess the Password

Computers usually have passwords to protect them from unauthorized use. There are twelve to fourteen characters in a strong password. A strong password includes upper and lowercase letters, numbers, and special characters.

Ruby's dad decided to change the password after Ruby's adventure. Help Ruby guess the new password based on the hints Dad left.

■ Small, redheaded girl with a big imagination

■ The first logic gate to pose a puzzle for Ruby

■ The small friend who helped Ruby throughout her journey

■ How many yellow notes are there above Dad's desk?

■ What special character can you spot on the uppermost note above Dad's desk?

Glossary

Application
A program that allows you to do a specific task, like write an e-mail. App is an abbreviation for application.

Bit
The smallest unit of data in computers. A bit can have only two values, which are often represented as either one or zero. A number system that uses only two digits is called binary. All computers calculate in binary.

Boolean
A type of data in computing that has only two possible answers, true or false.

Component
Also called a microchip or an integrated circuit. A set of electronic components like transistors on a chip. Computers are made from these chips.

Computer science
The study of the principles and practices of computer systems.

CPU
Central processing unit—the brains of the computer that processes program instructions.

Data
Units of information. In computing there can be different data types, including numbers, characters, and Booleans.

Electricity
Flow of electrons. In computers electricity helps turn the switches on and off.

GPU
Graphics Processing Unit. The component that helps manage video- and graphics-related requests.

Hardware
The physical parts of a computer system. For instance, the display, the components, and the keyboard.

Input device
A device that helps bring data into the computer, like a keyboard or a mouse.

Logic gate
Circuits that take several inputs, compare the inputs with each other, and provide a single output based on logical functions such as AND, OR, and NOT.

Machine language
Low-level code that is represented in binary numbers. The way computer hardware and the CPU understand instructions.

Mass storage
The hardware of a computer that stores data long-term, such as a memory card or hard drive.

Motherboard
The circuit board inside a computer that houses the CPU, memory, and connections to other devices.

Operating system
The software that manages the hardware and software resources in a computer system.

Output device
The devices that show the data a computer has processed in a human-understandable form, like a screen.

RAM
Random Access Memory. Memory that is constantly being written to and read from. When the computer is turned off, everything in RAM is lost.

ROM
Read Only Memory. Type of memory that has data stored on it that cannot be changed, like the booting instructions for the computer.

Sensor
Sensors detect events or changes in their environment and then provide an output. Sensors can measure, for example, temperature, light, or pressure.

Software
The programs, applications, and data in a computer system. Any parts of a computer system that aren't physical.

Transistor
Microscopic devices that open and close circuits to communicate electrical signals. CPUs contain millions of transistors.

User interface
The means by which a user interacts with a computer or device.

© Maija Tammi

Linda Liukas is a programmer, storyteller, and illustrator from Helsinki, Finland. *Hello Ruby*, her first children's book, made its debut on Kickstarter and quickly smashed its $10,000 funding goal after just 3.5 hours and gathering over $380,000 in total funding. To date the book has been translated into over twenty languages.

Linda is a central figure in the world of programming and worked on edutech before it was called that. Her TED Talk has gathered over one million views. Linda is the founder of Rails Girls, a global phenomenon teaching the basics of programming to young women all around the world. The workshops, organized by volunteers in over 260 cities, have taught more than 10,000 women the foundations of programming.

She previously worked at Codecademy, a programming education company in New York that boasts millions of users worldwide.

Further, she believes that code is the twenty-first-century literacy, and the need for people to speak the ABCs of programming is imminent. She believes our world is increasingly run by software and we need more diversity in the people who are building it. The best way to introduce programming to children is through compelling storytelling. Having never really outgrown fairy tales, she views the Web as a maze of stories and wants to hear more diverse voices in that world.

Linda has studied business, design, and engineering at Aalto University and product engineering at Stanford University. She was selected as the 2013 Ruby Hero (the most notable prize within the Ruby programming community), is the Digital Champion of Finland, appointed by EU commisioner Neelie Kroes, and she won the State Award for Children's Culture in 2014.

lindaliukas.fi
@lindaliukas
helloruby.com